A NOTE TO PARENTS

Reading Aloud with Your Child

Research shows that reading books aloud is the single most valuable support parents can provide in helping children learn to read.

- Be a ham! The more enthusiasm you display, the more your child will enjoy the book.
- Run your finger underneath the words as you read to signal that the print carries the story.
- Leave time for examining the illustrations more closely; encourage your child to find things in the pictures.
- Invite your youngster to join in whenever there's a repeated phrase in the text.
- Link up events in the book with similar events in your child's life.
- If your child asks a question, stop and answer it. The book can be a means to learning more about your child's thoughts.

Listening to Your Child Read Aloud

The support of your attention and praise is absolutely crucial to your child's continuing efforts to learn to read.

- If your child is learning to read and asks for a word, give it immediately so that the meaning of the story is not interrupted. DO NOT ask your child to sound out the word.
- On the other hand, if your child initiates the act of sounding out, don't intervene.
- If your child is reading along and makes what is called a miscue, listen for the sense of the miscue. If the word "road" is substituted for the word "street," for instance, no meaning is lost. Don't stop the reading for a correction.
- If the miscue makes no sense (for example, "horse" for "house"), ask your child to reread the sentence because you're not sure you understand what's just been read.
- Above all else, enjoy your child's growing command of print and make sure you give lots of praise. *You are your child's first teacher — and the most important one. Praise from you is critical for further risk-taking and learning.*

— Priscilla Lynch
Ph.D., New York University
Educational Consultant

To Bushman —
With apologies for last time

Text copyright © 1998 by Daniel Pinkwater.
Illustrations copyright © 1998 by Jill Pinkwater.
All rights reserved. Published by Scholastic Inc.
HELLO READER! and CARTWHEEL BOOKS and associated logos
are trademarks and/or registered trademarks of Scholastic Inc.

Library of Congress Cataloging-in-Publication Data

Pinkwater, Daniel Manus, 1941-
    Second-grade ape / by Daniel Pinkwater; illustrated by Jill
Pinkwater.
        p.   cm.—(Hello reader! Level 4)
    "Cartwheel Books."
    Summary: Flash Fleetwood finds a very quiet gorilla which he
names Phil, and to the delight of the second grade students, their
teacher Mrs. Hotdogbun says he may attend school along with them.
    ISBN 0-590-37261-0
    [1. Gorilla — Fiction. 2. Schools — Fiction. 3. Humorous stories.]
I. Pinkwater, Jill, ill. II. Title. III. Series.
PZ7.P6335Se   1997
[Fic] — dc21   97-13717
                                                                   CIP
                                                                   AC

10 9 8   0/0 01 02

Printed in the U.S.A.   24

First printing, February 1998

Second-Grade APE

by Daniel Pinkwater
Illustrated by Jill Pinkwater

Hello Reader! — Level 4

SCHOLASTIC INC.

New York   Toronto   London   Auckland   Sydney

CHAPTER 1

A VERY BIG CAT

Flash Fleetwood was walking in the woods behind his house, when he found an animal. It was quite a big animal. It was bigger than Flash Fleetwood. Flash Fleetwood was just walking along, and there it was, sitting under a bush, eating a leaf.

Flash Fleetwood watched the animal for a while. It sat quietly and watched him. It didn't seem to be afraid.

"What kind of animal is this?" Flash Fleetwood asked himself.

Maybe it is a cat, he thought. "Are you a cat?" he asked the animal.

"Whoop! Whoop! Whoop whoop whoop!" said the animal.

Flash Fleetwood had a chocolate chip cookie in his pocket.

"Here, cat. Do you want this cookie?" he asked. He held the cookie out to the animal.

The animal took the cookie and ate it slowly. He looked at Flash Fleetwood with eyes full of love.

I will take this cat home, Flash Fleetwood thought.

"Cat, do you want to come home with me?" he asked the animal.

"Whoop! Whoop!" the animal said.

"I think that means yes. Come on, cat."

Flash Fleetwood walked home through the woods. The animal followed him, tearing off branches as it went and whooping from time to time. Sometimes it would leap into the trees and swing from branch to branch.

Unusual cat, Flash Fleetwood thought.

Flash Fleetwood arrived at his house.

His father was outside. He was punishing the chickens.

"You chickens will stand facing the corner," Flash Fleetwood's father said, "until you learn it is wrong to make fun of humans."

"Hello, Freddie," his father said. "What have you been up to?"

Flash Fleetwood's real name was Freddie. His father never called him Flash. He always called him Freddie.

"Hello, Dad. See the big cat I found."

"That is no cat, Freddie. That is a gorilla," Flash Fleetwood's father said.

"Really?" Flash Fleetwood asked.

"I am sure of it," his father said.

"Will you let me keep him?" Flash Fleetwood asked.

"He might be a lost gorilla, Freddie," Flash Fleetwood's father said. "His owners might be looking for him. We will look in the newspaper and telephone the animal shelter. If no one is advertising for a lost gorilla, maybe — just maybe — you may keep him."

Then he called to Flash Fleetwood's mother, "Mother! Come and see Freddie's gorilla!"

Flash Fleetwood's mother came out of the kitchen door. She was mixing up a big bowl of lunch. She held the bowl in her arm, and mixed the lunch with a wooden spoon.

"My goodness! It really is a gorilla!" Flash Fleetwood's mother said.

"He thought it was a cat," Flash Fleetwood's father said.

"That boy!" Flash Fleetwood's mother said. "What will he bring home next? It is quite a nice gorilla, isn't it?"

Then she said, "Shall we let him keep it?"

"Why not?" Flash Fleetwood's father said. "If no one advertises for a lost gorilla for a week, and if no one has come looking for one at the animal shelter, we might let him keep it, don't you think?"

"It is quite a nice gorilla," Flash Fleetwood's mother said again. "We'll have to see. But now, come to lunch. It's egg salad pie and raw spinach. Do you think the gorilla will like that?"

The gorilla ate all the raw spinach.

"You thought he was a cat?" Flash Fleetwood's mother asked.

"Only at first," Flash Fleetwood said.

"He is much bigger than a cat," Flash Fleetwood's father said.

"It was dark where I found him," Flash Fleetwood said.

"He is twenty times bigger than a cat," Flash Fleetwood's mother said.

"Look, I made a mistake, OK?" Flash Fleetwood said.

"It is funny that you thought it was a cat," Flash Fleetwood's father said.

"Anybody can make a mistake," Flash Fleetwood said.

"Of course, dear," Flash Fleetwood's mother said.

"You were lucky to find a gorilla," his father said.

"May I show the gorilla to Bullets Birkenstock?" Flash Fleetwood asked his parents.

"He should have a bath first," Flash Fleetwood's mother said.

"Please. We'll come back soon," Flash Fleetwood said.

"Come back soon and give the gorilla a bath,"
Flash Fleetwood's mother said.

"I will," said Flash Fleetwood.

CHAPTER 2
BULLETS BIRKENSTOCK

Bullets Birkenstock was Flash Fleetwood's best friend. Bullets Birkenstock's real name was Bruce Birkenstock.

They made up their nicknames themselves.

Nobody but Bullets Birkenstock called Freddie Fleetwood "Flash" Fleetwood. Nobody else called him that.

Only Flash Fleetwood called Bruce Birkenstock "Bullets" Birkenstock. Nobody else called him that.

Bullets Birkenstock was smart. He was the smartest person Flash Fleetwood knew. He knew a lot about animals.

Bullets Birkenstock had a dog named Rolf. Bullets Birkenstock was teaching Rolf to talk. Already Rolf could say his name.

"What's your name?" Bullets Birkenstock would say.

"Rolf! Rolf!" Rolf would bark.

"See?" Bullets Birkenstock would say. "He said 'Rolf.' He can say his name."

Flash Fleetwood walked to Bullets Birkenstock's house. He led the gorilla by holding one of its fingers. Its fingers were the size of bananas. The gorilla walked behind Flash Fleetwood and shuffled its feet along the sidewalk.

"You are a nice, tame gorilla," Flash Fleetwood said.

The gorilla whooped to Flash Fleetwood.

They came to Bullets Birkenstock's house. Flash Fleetwood knocked on the door.

"Bullets Birkenstock, come out and see what I have!" Flash Fleetwood called.

Bullets Birkenstock came out.

"Leaping lollipops!" Bullets Birkenstock said. "Look at the size of that cat!"

"Leaping lollipops!" was something Bullets Birkenstock liked to say.

"Ha!" Flash Fleetwood said. "It is not a cat."

"It is not a cat? What is it?" Bullets Birkenstock asked.

"It is a gorilla," Flash Fleetwood said.

"Leaping lollipops!" Bullets Birkenstock said.

"Ha! You thought it was a cat," Flash Fleetwood said.

"Only at first," Bullets Birkenstock said. "You were standing in the shadows with it. It is a neat gorilla. I can see that now."

"Whoop! Whoop! Whoop whoop whoop!"
the gorilla said.

"Are they going to let you keep him?" Bullets
Birkenstock asked.

"Why not?" Flash Fleetwood said. "If nobody
advertises in the paper for a week, and if nobody
asks for him at the animal shelter, he is mine.
My gorilla. Finders keepers."

"Wow! Lucky! What is his name?" Bullets Birkenstock asked.

"His name is Phil," Flash Fleetwood said.

"Phil?" Bullets Birkenstock asked.

"Phil the gorilla," Flash Fleetwood said. "I made up my mind on the way over here."

"Let's have Phil meet Rolf," Bullets Birkenstock said.

Bullets Birkenstock called his dog.

Rolf saw Phil.

Phil saw Rolf.

"Whoop! Whoop! Whoop whoop whoop!" said Phil.

"Yipe!" said Rolf.

Rolf was afraid of Phil. He cringed. He cowered. He put his tail between his legs. He looked as though he wanted to run away, but wasn't sure what the gorilla would do if he did.

"Look, Rolf. He's a good gorilla," Bullets Birkenstock said.

Flash Fleetwood and Bullets Birkenstock patted Phil.

"See? Don't be scared of him," they said.

Phil said "Whoop!" very softly.

Rolf wagged his tail.

It was a very small wag.

Phil patted Rolf.

Rolf wagged his tail a little more. He still wasn't sure, but he wasn't quite so scared.

"Let's all go for a walk," Flash Fleetwood said.

"Let's walk in the woods," Bullets Birkenstock said.

"Woof," Rolf said.

"Whoop!" Phil said.

CHAPTER 3

IN THE WOODS

In the woods, Phil showed off his tricks.

He could climb very high. He could swing from tree to tree. He could fall, crashing through branches. And he could fall on his head. He never got hurt.

Phil could pick up big logs. He could run through the woods. He could whoop very loudly. He could pound on his chest. It sounded like a drum. He could eat leaves. He could pick up things with his feet.

Flash Fleetwood, Bullets Birkenstock, and Rolf were filled with admiration.

"He is the greatest gorilla who ever lived," Bullets Birkenstock said.

"Yes, he is," Flash Fleetwood said.

"Do you think, if you are ever sick, or have to go away, or if you die, Phil could stay at my house?" Bullets Birkenstock asked.

"If I am sick, or if I have to go away, or if I die, Phil can stay with you," Flash Fleetwood said. "You are my best friend."

"Could he stay at my house, just for one night, even if you don't die or anything?" Bullets Birkenstock asked.

"Maybe later," Flash Fleetwood said. "After he has settled down and gotten used to me. Maybe then."

"Wow," Bullets Birkenstock said.

Bullets Birkenstock had brought cookies.

The boys and the dog and the gorilla sat on a log. They each ate a cookie.

"You know, Phil is a neat animal," Bullets Birkenstock said.

"He sure is," Flash Fleetwood said. "I'm going to bring him to school tomorrow."

"Leaping lollipops!" said Bullets Birkenstock.

CHAPTER 4

BREAKFAST WITH A GORILLA

Flash Fleetwood asked his parents, "May I take my gorilla to school tomorrow?"

"Only if you give him a bath," Flash Fleetwood's mother said.

Giving a bath to a gorilla is a big project. It took more than an hour, and the bathroom got very wet. Flash Fleetwood had to clean the bathroom, too. And it took all the towels to get Phil dry.

"If you are going to have a pet, you have to take care of it," Flash Fleetwood's mother said.

"Where will Phil sleep?" Flash Fleetwood asked.

Flash Fleetwood's father had found a book about gorillas.

"Gorillas like to make nests to sleep in," Flash Fleetwood's father told him. "Sometimes a nest in a tree, and sometimes a nest on the ground. They like to feel protected."

Flash Fleetwood helped Phil make a nest of blankets in his closet. Phil liked it. He curled up and went to sleep.

In the morning, Phil was not in his nest. Flash Fleetwood ran downstairs. Phil was in the kitchen with his mother and father. They were eating pancakes. Flash Fleetwood ate some, too. Flash Fleetwood's mother ate some. Flash Fleetwood's father ate a lot of pancakes. Phil the gorilla ate a great many pancakes. He ate more than twenty pancakes. He used all the maple syrup. He drank six glasses of milk. He ate five bananas, which were all the bananas in the house. He ate two apples. He ate an orange.

"Phil has a good appetite," Flash Fleetwood's father said.

"It will be expensive, shopping for a gorilla," Flash Fleetwood's mother said.

"Oh, pancakes don't cost very much," Flash Fleetwood's father said.

CHAPTER 5

SECOND-GRADE APE

Flash Fleetwood and Phil got to school early. Flash Fleetwood left Phil in the hall and went into his classroom.

His teacher was Mrs. Hotdogbun. She always came to school early.

"Mrs. Hotdogbun, I brought my pet to school," Flash Fleetwood said.

"We do not bring pets to school, Freddie," Mrs. Hotdogbun said.

"It is an unusual pet," Flash Fleetwood said. "I thought I would show it to the class."

"Oh. Unusual pets are different," Mrs. Hotdogbun said. "But you should have asked first."

"I asked my mother. She said it would be all right," Flash Fleetwood said.

"Well, in that case, I am sure it will be all right," Mrs. Hotdogbun said. "Is it a mouse? Some children have mice as pets."

"No, it is not a mouse," Flash Fleetwood said.

"Is it a lizard?" Mrs. Hotdogbun asked. "I like lizards very much."

"No, it is not a lizard," Flash Fleetwood said.

"Is it a fish?" Mrs. Hotdogbun asked. "Fish make very nice pets."

"No," said Flash Fleetwood. "It is not a fish."

"What sort of pet is it?" Mrs. Hotdogbun asked.

"My pet is in the hall," Flash Fleetwood said. "I will bring it in."

Flash Fleetwood went out to the hall.
Phil was looking at the drawings on the walls.
He brought Phil into the classroom.
"This is Phil," Flash Fleetwood said.
"Eeek!" Mrs. Hotdogbun said.
"Whoop!" Phil said.
"That is a GORILLA!"
"Yes!" said Flash Fleetwood. "Bullets
Birkenstock thought it was a cat."
  "Whoop!" said Phil.

"Freddie, is this a tame gorilla? Is he gentle?"

"He is tame. He is gentle," Flash Fleetwood said.

"I hope so," said Mrs. Hotdogbun. "I sincerely hope so."

"Phil is the finest gorilla who ever lived," Flash Fleetwood said.

"Your gorilla must sit in my own personal closet," Mrs. Hotdogbun said. "He must sit there and be very quiet. Can he do that?"

"Yes," said Flash Fleetwood. "He sat in my closet all night. He was very quiet."

"Has the gorilla had a bath?" Mrs. Hotdogbun asked.

"Yes," said Flash Fleetwood. "He had a bath last night."

"Good," said Mrs. Hotdogbun. "I will tell you when it is time to show him to the children."

Flash Fleetwood took Phil to the closet.
"Now sit here, and be very quiet," Flash
Fleetwood said.
"Whoop," said Phil quietly.

The children came in and took their seats.
Bullets Birkenstock was with them.

"Where's Phil?" Bullets Birkenstock asked
Flash Fleetwood.

"Wait," Flash Fleetwood said.

"Class," Mrs. Hotdogbun said, "Freddie
has brought his unusual pet to show us."

"Not another mouse!" someone shouted.

"Is it a lizard?" someone else shouted. "I hate lizards."

"It had better not be a boring fish, Freddie!" someone else shouted.

"Hush!" Mrs. Hotdogbun said. "Freddie, you may go to my closet and get your pet."

Freddie went to Mrs. Hotdogbun's closet.

He took Phil by the finger and led him out.

"Yaaaaaay!" the children shouted.

"This is my pet," Flash Fleetwood said.

"Yaaaaaay!"

"His name is Phil."

"Yaaaaaay!"

"He is a gorilla."

"Yaaaaaay!"

"Mrs. Hotdogbun, if we take Phil outside he can do some tricks on the jungle gym," Flash Fleetwood said.

"We will put our coats on now," Mrs. Hotdogbun said. "We will go outside and watch Phil. We will go quietly through the halls."

"Yaaaaaay!" the children shouted quietly.

Outside, Phil did some tricks on the jungle gym.

After doing his tricks, Phil came back to the classroom.

He sat in the back of the room. He sat there for the rest of the day. Mrs. Hotdogbun gave Phil some paints. He painted some pictures.

She gave him an orange. He ate the orange. He was very quiet. He was no trouble at all.

At the end of the day, Mrs. Hotdogbun said, "Phil is a very good gorilla. He is quiet. He is no trouble at all."

"Could Phil come back tomorrow?" some children asked. "Could Phil come to school every day?"

"Yes!" the children shouted. "Let Phil come to school every day."

"Let Phil be in our class!"

"But, children, Phil is a gorilla," Mrs. Hotdogbun said.

"He is a very good gorilla!"
"He is no trouble at all."
"You said so yourself!"
"Please, Mrs. Hotdogbun! Let Phil come
to school every day!" the children shouted.
"Let him be in our class!"
"Please?"
"Well," Mrs. Hotdogbun said. "Why not?"